Genies
Don't Ride
Bicycles

There are more books about the Bailey School Kids!
Have you read these adventures?

Vampires Don't Wear Polka Dots
Santa Claus Doesn't Mop Floors
Leprechauns Don't Play Basketball
Werewolves Don't Go to Summer Camp
Ghosts Don't Eat Potato Chips
Frankenstein Doesn't Plant Petunias
Aliens Don't Wear Braces

Genies Don't Ride Bicycles

by Debbie Dadey
and
Marcia Thornton Jones

Illustrated by John Steven Gurney

A
LITTLE APPLE
PAPERBACK

SCHOLASTIC INC.
New York Toronto London Auckland Sydney

No part of this publication may be reproduced in whole or in part, or stored in a retrieval system, or transmitted in any form or by any means, electronic, mechanical, photocopying, recording, or otherwise, without written permission of the publisher. For information regarding permission, write to Scholastic Inc., 730 Broadway, New York, NY 10003.

ISBN 0-590-47297-6

23 22 21 20 19 18 17 16 15 14 13   7 8/9

Printed in the U.S.A.   40

First Scholastic printing, November 1993

Book design by Laurie McBarnette

To Robert Edwin Thornton and Voline "Bonnie" Gibson.
Thanks for the bike rides
and bringing magic into our lives.

Contents

1

The Bottle

"What is it?" Melody asked Eddie. "Let me see."

"Keep your pigtails glued on," Eddie told her. "It's stuck." Eddie, Melody, and their friends Howie and Liza were in their favorite meeting place under the big oak tree on the school playground. The sun shone bright in the blue December sky, but none of the kids paid any attention. It was the first time they had noticed a strange object sticking out from a crack between two branches of the tree. Eddie tugged as hard as he could, but it didn't move.

Liza flung her blonde hair over her shoulder. "Maybe it's buried treasure."

"In a tree?" Eddie laughed.

1

"Let me help," Howie offered. Together the two boys tugged. All at once the object broke free and they fell backwards onto the ground.

Eddie held the object in his hands. "It's just an old bottle," he sighed as he looked at the slick green bottle. It had strange words scribbled across the side and a big gold stopper.

"Why don't you open it?" Liza asked. "Maybe someone put a secret message inside and it's been hidden for hundreds of years."

"If it's been hidden there for hundreds of years then why haven't we seen it before?" Eddie asked.

Melody nodded. "We're here every day after school. There's no way we could have missed it."

"It was hidden in that crack. Last night's windstorm probably loosened the tree limb," Howie suggested.

"If you're not going to open it, then

give it to me." Melody reached for the bottle.

"I'll open it." Eddie pulled on the gold stopper. It didn't budge. He sat down on the ground and put the bottle between his legs. He pulled again with all his strength.

POP!

"Pew-whee! What's that smell?" Liza complained.

Eddie stood up and held the bottle toward his friends. "It's this old bottle.

There's nothing in it except a sewer smell." He threw the bottle and the stopper into the yard next to the school.

"You shouldn't litter," Liza told him.

Eddie shrugged. "There's nothing in that yard but junk. One more stinky bottle won't make a difference."

The four kids looked at the yard behind the oak tree. A broken wooden fence surrounded flat tires, broken bottles, and metal barrels.

"It sure is ugly." Liza shivered and pulled on her mittens. "Especially when the other houses have bright Christmas lights."

"I wish someone would clean up this place," Melody said.

"You might as well wish for a million dollars," Eddie told her. "No one's lived in that dump for years."

Melody sighed. "You're right. But it never hurts to wish."

2

Holiday Spirit

"I can't believe it!" Howie shouted. "It was a junkyard yesterday." He was the first one to reach the oak tree the next day before school.

Melody trotted up beside him and stared. "It's a miracle!"

"It's a miracle Mrs. Jeepers hasn't driven me crazy. I thought I'd never finish my science homework." Eddie shook his head as he and Liza walked up to the oak tree. Mrs. Jeepers was their strict third-grade teacher.

"Mrs. Jeepers is nothing compared to this." Melody pointed to the yard next to the school. Yesterday the yard had been filled with trash, but today not a speck of broken glass or old tires remained.

Even the green bottle was gone. Now the grass was neatly trimmed and the fence was straight and covered with Christmas lights. Bright strands of lights were strung on the railing of the back porch and were draped around every tree and bush in the yard.

Liza had a long woolen scarf wrapped around her neck so only her nose and eyes could be seen. "It looks great," she said.

"It's great for the electric company," Eddie laughed. "Whoever hung those lights is going to have a doozie of an electric bill."

"I guess Melody was right," Liza said. "It never hurts to make a wish."

Howie looked at his friends. "Don't you think it's odd that this junkyard was cleaned up overnight?"

"I think it's wonderful," Liza said through her scarf.

Just then a big man with a shiny bald

head rode a purple bicycle into the yard behind the house. Muscles bulged under his gold brocade vest and bright, flowing orange pants covered his legs. Gold necklaces hung around his neck and one ear had a gold earring dangling from it. He honked the bicycle's horn and waved at the four friends. "How do you do?" he sang out in a deep voice.

"J . . . just fine, thank you," Howie answered. "How are you?"

The big man laughed a deep friendly laugh. "Today, I am fine. As a matter of fact, today I am wonderful. It's been ages since I've gotten any exercise."

"I haven't seen you around before," Eddie said suspiciously.

The man smiled. "I breezed in yesterday."

Liza reached out her hand. "My name is Liza. It's very nice to meet you."

The man leaned his bike against the fence and reached to kiss Liza's hand.

"My name is Eugene and it is my pleasure to serve such a lovely fair-haired lady."

Liza giggled. "You sure made this yard sparkle."

When the stranger laughed his teeth shone next to his dark skin. "I've been cooped up for such a long time it felt good to work in the fresh air."

Liza nodded. "I bet the rest of the neighbors will be glad! Finally this house has some holiday spirit!"

"I wish we didn't have to go to school," Eddie muttered as the school bell rang. "Then I'd have some holiday spirit, too."

As they turned to leave, Liza waved at Eugene. "We'll see you later," she said.

Eugene bowed. "Your wish is my command." His deep laughter echoed across the playground and followed the kids into the school.

3

Blizzard

Mrs. Jeepers, their third-grade teacher, rubbed her green brooch as Eddie, Liza, Melody, and Howie rushed to their seats.

"We're sorry to be late," Melody said.

Howie nodded. "We were just admiring the new neighbor's holiday decorations."

Mrs. Jeepers' green eyes flashed in their direction. "We do not have time to waste on twinkling lights." Mrs. Jeepers had a strange accent and spoke very softly. She didn't need to shout because the kids in her class always paid attention. If they didn't, she rubbed her brooch and her green eyes flashed. Then strange things would happen. Some kids even believed she was a vampire.

By the time Mrs. Jeepers loaded them down with work, the kids had forgotten all about the new neighbor. They were busy with fifty math problems and two science experiments.

Halfway through the morning, Howie blew on his hands to warm them, and Liza's teeth started chattering. Mrs. Jeepers pulled on a sweater and checked the thermostat.

"It's too cold in here to work," Melody whispered.

Eddie shrugged. "It's not so bad. It never gets real cold in Bailey City." But Eddie was wrong. By the end of the day, thick gray clouds rolled over the city, and ice formed on the windows of the school.

"Maybe it'll snow," Melody whispered as they turned in their English assignments.

Howie shook his head. "Bailey City has not had a decent snow in years.

Besides, I heard the weather report on the radio this morning. It is going to be sunny and mild today."

"Maybe in Hawaii, but it definitely looks like snow for Bailey City!" Eddie pointed out the window. Huge soft snowflakes drifted down and stuck to the bare branches of the old oak tree.

By the end of the school day, a white rug of snow completely covered the ground, and the big oak tree's branches looked like sticks with white cotton candy.

Eugene honked his bicycle horn when the kids rushed out of the school door. "How do you like the snow?" he asked, parking his bike. He was still dressed in his vest and flowing pants.

"It's beautiful!" Melody laughed and stuck out her hand to catch a snowflake.

Liza put on her hat and wrapped a scarf around her face as the kids slid across the playground. "We'd better hurry

home. The streets are going to get slippery."

"Great." Eddie skated on the slick snow behind Eugene's house. "The roads will be bad, and school will be canceled!"

"You will be in the holiday spirit now," Eugene hollered to Eddie.

Howie froze right in the middle of a step. "Did you hear that?" he asked.

"All I hear is Liza's teeth chattering," Eddie told him.

"I meant what Eugene said," Howie hissed. "It's what Eddie wished for."

"What are you talking about?" Melody asked.

"Eddie wished for no school."

"So, why complain?" Eddie asked.

"I'll tell you why," Melody interrupted. "Harry Headbanger and his band are supposed to play for us tomorrow. We'll miss it if the snow doesn't melt."

"That's just great," Eddie grumbled. "One good thing happens all year and we'll miss it because of this stupid snow."

Eugene kicked through the snow with his funny green boots and leaned on the fence. "Why so glum, my young friends? You said you did not want to go to school and it looks like your wish will come true."

"Usually I don't want to go to school," Eddie muttered. "But I'd do just about anything to see a Harry Headbanger concert."

"School wouldn't be so bad if it weren't for Mrs. Jeepers," Melody added.

"She's not always mean," Liza said softly. "After all, she did ask Harry Headbanger to play at school tomorrow."

"I wish this snow would melt tonight," Howie said. "Then we wouldn't miss the concert."

"I wish Mrs. Jeepers weren't so mean," Eddie added, "then I wouldn't mind school so much."

None of the kids paid much attention as Eugene began to laugh.

4

Heat Wave

"This is one day I'm glad there was school," Eddie said to his friends as he sank into his seat the next day. "I can't wait for the concert." The morning bell had not yet rung, and Mrs. Jeepers was already writing assignments on the board. There were puddles on the classroom floor, and several buckets sat around the room to catch water from the leaking roof.

Howie nodded and looked out the window. The sun was shining bright, turning yesterday's mountain of snow into ponds of water. "But this crazy weather sure has made a mess. Most of Bailey City is flooded."

"I don't care, I'm just glad the snow

melted," Melody told him. "The concert will be fantastic."

Mrs. Jeepers turned around quickly, causing her purple polka-dotted skirt to swirl. "I am sorry, students. The principal informed me this morning that because of the flood, Harry Headbanger and his band will not be able to perform for us today. Their instruments were damaged from all the water."

"They don't have to play instruments," Melody told her. "They could just sing."

"We'll tap our feet, and Eddie can play his comb," Liza begged.

"That is very thoughtful of you, but the group has already canceled," Mrs. Jeepers explained and continued writing on the board.

"That stupid snow has caused nothing but trouble," Eddie complained.

"You're the one who wished for no school," Melody pointed out.

"Then you wished the snow would

melt," Liza reminded Howie.

"And *it did!*" Howie called out.

"So what?" Eddie muttered. "We're still missing the concert."

"Don't you think it's strange that both of our wishes came true?" Howie asked.

"My wish did, too," Melody pointed out. "I wished for that junkyard to be cleaned up."

"So?" Eddie said softly. "I wished that Mrs. Jeepers would be nice and that hasn't come true. Just look at all the work she's putting on the board."

The four kids looked at their teacher just as she dropped a piece of chalk. "I cannot work in these miserable conditions. Even the chalk is wet. There is no use trying to work today," she told her surprised students. "Let us spend the day watching videos and playing games."

Several students cheered, but Melody gulped and looked at Howie as they remembered Eddie's wish. "Mrs. Jeepers never lets us watch a video," Melody whispered.

"Shall we make it a party?" Mrs. Jeepers continued. "I will have some cookies sent in."

Eddie hollered out, "Can we have ice cream, too?" The rest of the class grew silent. Mrs. Jeepers hated for anyone to yell in her class. But her eyes didn't flash and she didn't rub her brooch. She smiled a big toothy grin instead of her usual odd little half smile.

"Certainly," Mrs. Jeepers said.

"It looks like all our wishes have come true," Howie said when they reached the oak tree after school.

"Wishes just don't come true like that. I've wished for plenty of things and they didn't come true," Eddie argued.

"That's right," Melody agreed. "Nobody can make wishes come true."

"Nobody, except a genie in a magic bottle." Liza giggled.

"That's it!" Howie shouted. "Remember the green bottle we found?"

Liza jumped up and down. "That must have been a genie's bottle, and we let him out. That's why our wishes are coming true!"

"Then where is the genie?" Melody asked.

The four kids heard a bicycle horn as Eugene rode into his backyard and waved. Melody and Howie waved back. But Liza's eyes were big as she pointed.

"There's the genie. You just waved at him."

"Liza, you've popped your cork," Eddie teased. "Genies are only in fairy tales. Besides, they don't ride purple bicycles. They fly on magic carpets."

"Don't be so sure that Liza's crazy," Howie told him. "Remember that Eugene showed up right after we opened the bottle."

"He sure looks like a genie," Melody agreed.

"And his name is EUGENE," Liza said.

Eddie laughed. "The next thing you know, you'll have Arabians on horseback taking over Bailey City. There's no such thing as a genie. After all, if I could do magic, I'd be better-looking than him."

"Shh, he'll hear you," Liza warned Eddie.

"Who cares?" Eddie bellowed. "What's he going to do? Wish me into Aladdin's

lamp? You guys are stupid to believe slush like that."

"I wish you'd shut up," Melody snapped at Eddie. She was about to punch him in the arm when the kids heard booming laughter from the yard next door.

Melody's eyes got big and she whispered, "Oh my gosh, what have I done?"

5

Croak

Eddie trudged across the muddy playground the next morning as his three friends waited under the oak tree.

"I guess we were silly to think Eugene is a genie," Howie said. "Eddie had plenty to say yesterday, even after you made that wish."

"You're right," Melody laughed. "No one can make Eddie shut up."

Eddie stopped in front of his friends and glared at Melody. "What's wrong?" Melody asked.

Eddie opened his mouth to answer. But all that came out was a sickly croak.

"Are you sick?" Liza asked.

"CROAK!" Eddie said again.

Melody's eyes got big. "Oh, no! My wish did come true."

"It's just laryngitis," Howie said.

Eddie nodded. Then he croaked some more. This time his friends could tell what he was saying. "Grandma gave me this terrible medicine. She said I'll be fine in a few days. It has nothing to do with that stupid wish."

"But you can barely talk," Melody pointed out.

Howie nodded and looked at their neighbor's house. Eugene waved to them from his porch. Howie waved back and then whispered to his friends, "The weird weather could have made Eddie lose his voice."

"Or it could have been Melody's wish," Liza interrupted.

"Shhh," Howie warned. "From now on, we need to be very careful not to let Eugene hear us. And no more wishing! Just in case he is a genie."

Eddie shook his head and squeaked, "I can prove he's no genie."

"How?" Melody asked.

"I'll just make a wish," Eddie croaked. "I wish—"

Howie slapped his hand over Eddie's mouth with a loud smack. Eddie tried to get free, but Howie held on tight.

"Maybe Eddie's right for once," Melody said slowly. "The only way to know for sure is to make another wish. But it must be for something unusual so we know it's not just a coincidence."

Howie dropped his hand, and Eddie glared at him. "And something we really want," Eddie squawked.

"I've got it!" Liza yelled before her friends could stop her. "I wish for French fries, pizza, and chocolate candy for lunch every day!"

They looked at Eugene to see if he had heard. Goose bumps ran down their backs as he bowed and then continued polishing his purple bicycle.

6

Junk Food

"That was a stupid wish," Melody snapped as they headed inside the school. "Why didn't you wish for something good?"

"I did!" Liza cried. "Pizza and chocolate are good."

Eddie put his hands on his hips and croaked, "Those cafeteria ladies would never let us have junk food for lunch every day. I'm telling you there is no such thing as genies, especially in Bailey City."

But Eddie was wrong about lunch. As soon as the bell rang, Mrs. Jeepers cleared her throat and said, "There is some bad news. The food delivery truck has broken down. The cafeteria cannot serve the

31

chicken-and-broccoli bake that was on the menu."

"Too bad," Eddie said hoarsely.

"What are we having for lunch today?" Melody asked.

Mrs. Jeepers shook her head. "I am sure the cafeteria workers will come up with something good."

"That would be a real change," muttered Eddie.

By lunchtime, Liza was starved. "I can't wait for the pizza," she told Melody.

"You don't know we're having pizza," Melody said. "We'll probably end up with fish sticks."

Liza shook her head. "All your wishes came true. So will mine."

Everyone at Bailey Elementary was surprised to find the cafeteria serving their favorite foods. Everyone, that is, except Howie, Liza, Melody, and Eddie.

"Having our own personal genie might

not be so bad," Liza giggled as she bit into a slice of pizza.

"This still doesn't prove anything," Eddie croaked, and squirted ketchup on his French fries. "Delivery trucks can break down any time. It's not magic."

"Well, I'm glad it did today," Melody said. Then she took her tray back for a second helping of everything.

They were stuffed by the time they

finished. "I couldn't eat another bite," Howie moaned.

"I never want to see another chocolate bar in my whole life," Melody added. There were at least fifteen candy wrappers scattered on their table.

Eddie burped. "I feel terrible. I don't even want to go out for recess."

Liza nodded. "We could just rest by the oak tree."

Melody held her stomach and groaned as the kids sprawled under the oak tree at recess. "Maybe having our own genie isn't so great."

"We don't have a genie," Eddie squeaked.

"But my wish came true!" Liza argued. "That proves Eugene is a genie!"

"That doesn't prove anything," Eddie said roughly.

"It *is* hard to explain why the delivery truck broke down on the same day Liza made her wish," Howie said.

"So what?" Eddie said. "After all, my dad's truck hardly ever works."

Howie pointed to a snazzy red sports car as it drove by the playground. "Your dad ought to have that."

"Wow! I wish my dad had that car!" Eddie blurted out.

Before they could bat an eye, the sports car screeched to a stop, and Eddie's father stepped out.

7

Hocus-Pocus

"That's really a neat car your dad has," Howie said the next morning before school. The four friends were gathered under the oak tree on the warm December day.

"I'd love to zip around in that," Melody agreed.

Eddie frowned and muttered, "Dad just got it because he has to go out of town on business."

"But it's almost Christmas," Liza said.

"My dad doesn't give a jingle bell about Christmas," Eddie snapped.

"Maybe if you make a wish the genie will change things," Melody suggested.

Eddie kicked a puddle of mud and splashed the oak tree. "I don't believe in that hocus-pocus. I still say you're crazy."

"You could be wrong," Howie told him. He unzipped his blue bookbag and pulled out a large book. "I went to the public library last night and found this."

"You must be a genius." Eddie slapped his forehead. "You found a book in a library."

Howie ignored Eddie and opened the book. He showed his friends the section called *Genies: A Wish Come True.*

"Look at the picture!" Melody said. The kids looked at a large picture of a genie coming out of a green bottle. The genie looked exactly like Eugene.

No one said anything as Howie read. "'Genies may be held captive in bottles for thousands of years. The legend says that anyone, young or old, who frees a genie from his entrapment in a bottle shall be granted three wishes. The genie is then free from the curse of the bottle

and no more wishes shall be forth-coming.'"

"Fantastic!" Melody yelled. "There's four of us with three wishes each. That's twelve wishes!"

"We could wish for a whole toy store if we want," Liza laughed.

Howie closed the book and put it back in his backpack. "I think we'd better be careful what we wish for."

"I think you all need therapy," Eddie stomped in the mud puddle again.

"It's worth a try," Liza shrugged. She watched as Eugene pedaled into his back-yard. He honked his bicycle horn and waved. As he hopped off his purple bike and leaned it against the back porch, Liza said, "I wish I had a lifetime supply of bubble gum."

"I wish we could stay up all night," Howie said. "And I wish my mom wouldn't fuss at me."

"Is that the best you can do?" Eddie

asked. "Now this is a good wish . . . I wish for a million bucks."

Liza shook her head. "We ought to wish for something to help the world. I wish people would be nice to each other."

The school bell kept them from making any more wishes and from noticing Eugene smiling in their direction.

8

The *Nice* Surprise

"I had a great time," Howie told Eddie as they walked to school the next day.

"You should stay over every night," Eddie agreed.

Melody and Liza walked up behind them. "What are you guys talking about?" Melody asked.

"Howie spent the night with me last night and we played video games until one in the morning," Eddie explained.

Melody looked at Howie. "I can't believe your mom let you sleep over on a school night. She's usually so strict."

Howie nodded. "She was really weird yesterday. She didn't even fuss about my room being a mess."

The four friends reached the steps in

front of Bailey Elementary. Eddie and Howie sat down on the top step.

"My mom was nice yesterday, too," Liza told them. "She took me shopping and bought me five new outfits. The lady in the store was so happy, she gave us an extra dress for free!"

"It must be *Be Nice to Kids Week*," Eddie said. "I thought my dad would bust a gut when I splattered blue paint all over his new red car, but he just shrugged and helped me wipe it off. It was eerie!"

Just then Carey, a girl from their class, stopped at the bottom of the steps. "Did you study for the science test?" she asked. "I studied for three hours!"

Liza's eyes got big. "I forgot all about the test. I was too busy trying on my new clothes."

Melody sighed. "I couldn't study. All this melting snow damaged our roof, and water was dripping everywhere. My science book got soaked."

"We studied," Howie told them.

Eddie nodded. "Right after we finished playing video games."

"Eddie studied?" Melody gasped. "That's a first."

"I bet I get the highest grade in the class," Carey bragged and climbed the steps. Just when she reached the top step, she stumbled and fell backwards. Melody caught her, but Carey's books and papers flew everywhere. Before Carey could mutter a sound, Eddie hopped up and dashed after her homework. He caught all the papers before they blew away.

Eddie handed the papers to Carey. "You have to watch that top step. Are you okay?"

Carey blushed. "I think so. Thanks for picking up my stuff."

"No problem." Eddie shrugged and held the door open until Carey was inside. When he faced his friends, they were

staring at him with their mouths wide open.

"What's wrong with you?" he asked.

Melody slowly shook her head. "Life at Bailey Elementary will never be the same. First Eddie studies for a test, and then he's actually nice to someone."

"To Carey!" Howie added. "I thought you didn't like Carey."

Eddie's face turned as red as his hair. "Just because I was nice doesn't mean I like her," he snapped.

"*Nice!*" Liza shrieked. "Don't you know what's happened? Everyone's being nice!"

Howie patted Liza on the back. "There's nothing wrong with that."

Liza looked at each of her friends. "But people are being too nice. Don't you remember our wishes? I wished for people to be *nice* to each other."

The four kids were quiet as they thought about their wishes from the day before.

Then Eddie said, "People can be nice without a genie's magic."

"Sure they can," Melody agreed. "When our minister was sick, we all took turns bringing him hot meals."

"But what about Eddie's dad and Howie's mom? Isn't it strange for them to suddenly be nice right after I made my wish?" Liza asked.

"My dad's been nice before," Eddie said. "He even took me camping once."

"And my mom isn't *that* bad," Howie added.

Liza put her hands on her hips. "Well, I've never gotten a free dress before and I've never seen Eddie be that nice to anyone!"

"Liza's right," Melody said slowly. "Liza's wish *did* come true, so Eugene must be a genie."

"So what are we going to do about Eugene?" Howie asked as he led his friends into the school.

Melody yawned. "I'm too tired to think about genies. After our roof started leaking last night, I didn't get a wink of sleep."

"We were up late, too," Eddie told her. "You don't hear us complaining."

"I couldn't sleep either," Liza said softly. "None of us slept. It's what Howie wished."

"It really is true," Melody said. "Eugene is a genie!"

"Hogwash," Eddie snapped. "Just because we got to stay up late doesn't mean the new neighbor is a bottled magician. After all, I didn't get my wish for a million bucks, and Liza hasn't gotten her bubble gum."

"Then explain why you were nice to Carey?" Howie demanded.

Eddie didn't get a chance to answer because Mrs. Jeepers interrupted them.

9

A Sticky Situation

Mrs. Jeepers stood in the doorway and smiled a big cheerful smile. "Come in, children."

"That smile gives me the creeps," Melody whispered as they went into the room. "It's not natural."

Liza shrugged. "She has to be nice. It was my wish."

Instead of her usual skirt and blouse, Mrs. Jeepers had on blue jeans, sneakers, and a Santa sweatshirt. Her green brooch was pinned to a Santa's hat. "We had such a wonderful time yesterday with our little party," she said, "I decided I did not want it to end." Mrs. Jeepers pulled a bag of bubble gum from her desk drawer and began passing it around. "Shall we

49

have a bubble blowing contest today?"

All the kids in the third grade cheered except for Howie and Melody. They were stunned. "This proves it," Howie said to Eddie.

Eddie shook his head as most of the class gathered around Mrs. Jeepers for their bubble gum. "What about my million bucks?"

Howie thought for a minute. "You wished for snow, for Mrs. Jeepers to be nice, and for that red sports car for your dad. That's three wishes. That's all you get."

Eddie kicked the chair in front of him. "That's not fair. I need one more wish."

"Then you *do* believe Eugene's a genie," Melody said.

"I believe I can blow the biggest bubble," Eddie snapped and ran up to get his gum.

They blew bubbles all morning. Eddie proved he was the best bubble blower in the third grade. He was so good, even Mrs. Jeepers asked for a demonstration. Eddie chewed a new wad of gum until it was soft. Then he blew and blew and blew until the bubble was as big as a basketball.

"That's incredible," Carey giggled and winked at Eddie.

"Too bad you have to pop it," Howie said.

But Eddie didn't pop it. He took the gum out of his mouth and held it up like a balloon. Unfortunately, it caught some of Liza's hair. Liza jerked away, but not soon enough. Eddie's prizewinning bubble popped right on top of her head.

"Look what you've done!" Liza screamed. She started pulling on the gooey strands, but the gum was stuck. "What am I going to do?"

Mrs. Jeepers stood over Liza and Eddie. The class held their breaths waiting for her eyes to glow and for her brooch to work its magic. Instead, Mrs. Jeepers smiled again. "What an unfortunate accident. We will have to cut the gum from your hair. But do not worry, your hair will grow back."

"Here are some scissors," Melody said.

Eddie grabbed the scissors. "I made the mess, I'll fix it."

"*No!*" Liza screamed. But she was too late. Eddie had already snipped off a hunk of hair.

"Hold still," Eddie told her. "I've almost got it all."

Liza whimpered as another hunk of hair fell into her lap. "I hate you," she screamed at Eddie. Then she threw her chewed wad of bubble gum. She aimed at Eddie. But it landed on the chalkboard beside Mrs. Jeepers instead. The entire class froze, even Liza.

Mrs. Jeepers plucked the gum from the chalkboard and wrapped it in a tissue. Howie gulped, and Melody closed her eyes when Mrs. Jeepers faced Liza.

"You are upset by this sticky situation," Mrs. Jeepers said very softly. "Perhaps some time out in the principal's office will help."

Liza's hands shook, and her face turned milk-white. "B. . .b. . .but I've n. . .n. . . never been sent to the principal's office before."

"Then it's high time you went," Eddie said.

"I believe Eddie is correct," Mrs. Jeepers added.

Melody shook her head. "You agree with Eddie?"

"Certainly," Mrs. Jeepers said. "Liza, please go."

The rest of the class stared as Liza slowly left the room. None of them felt like blowing bubbles anymore.

"Let us take our science test now," Mrs. Jeepers said. "Then we will be able to enjoy the afternoon."

The class groaned as Mrs. Jeepers passed out the papers. Howie yawned. "I wish we'd slept last night, but at least we studied."

Melody yawned, too. "I've never taken a test without studying."

Eddie grinned. "I'm a pro at it."

Howie and Melody put their heads down as Mrs. Jeepers gave out the directions. By the time she was finished, they were fast asleep.

10

Nutty

Howie pushed his tray of pizza and chocolate candy to the center of the lunchroom table. "I can't eat this junk again," he said. "My stomach is still churning from all that gum."

Eddie nodded. "My jaws are too sore to eat."

"I never thought I'd be sick of pizza," Melody admitted.

"I never thought I'd get sent to the principal's office," Liza said with tears in her eyes.

Howie patted her back. "You'll get over it. But what about Melody and me?"

Melody nodded. "This has been a terrible day. We slept straight through the test. And it's all Howie's fault."

"My fault?" Howie exclaimed. "What did I do?"

"You made the wish to stay up all night," Melody reminded him.

Liza held up her hand. "It wasn't Howie's fault, it's Eugene's."

"What did Eugene do?" Eddie asked.

"He made the wishes come true," Liza said.

Melody shook her head. "We made the wishes. It's our fault. Not Eugene's."

"Melody's right," Liza said. "And it's up to us to fix things."

"You're as nutty as peanut butter," Eddie laughed. "There's no way you can fix failing a test. Believe me, I know. We can't fix Liza's hair, either."

They looked at Liza. Short yellow spikes stuck out from the back of her head. "It doesn't look that bad," Melody said softly.

"I'll tell you what's bad," Howie said. "It's this heat wave. The snow is melting off Ruby Mountain. The river is rising and if it's not stopped, Bailey City will be flooded—just in time for Christmas."

"That's awful," Liza groaned. "People will be homeless for the holidays."

Howie nodded his head. "And that's just the beginning . . . there's a severe storm heading our way. That means even more flooding unless we do something about it."

"We should use our leftover wishes to

make things better," Liza suggested.

"Liza's right," Melody said.

"I don't have any wishes left," Eddie reminded them.

"I've used all three of mine, too," Howie said.

Liza nodded her head. "Me, too."

"I've just made two wishes," Melody told them. "One was for Eddie to shut up, which didn't last long enough, and the other was for the yard to be clean."

Howie put his hand on Melody's shoulder. "It's up to you. You're the only one who can save Bailey City from flooding."

"Oh, Melody," Liza whispered, "can you do it?"

Melody swallowed slowly and said, "I'll do it."

11

Don't Blow It!

After school the four kids rushed to the oak tree and looked into the stranger's yard. Christmas lights still blinked on the fence and tree. Mean clouds darkened the sky overhead and thunder rumbled nearby. Howie grabbed Melody's arm. "It's now or never," he told her.

"But it's going to storm. We'll get wet."

"More people will get wet if you don't," Liza told her.

"I think you're all soggy," Eddie said.

Melody took a deep breath. "Howie and Liza are right. We have to keep Bailey City from flooding."

"Be careful what you wish for," Liza whispered to Melody.

"Yeah," Eddie muttered, "don't blow it!"

Melody nodded her head and called out, "Eugene, can we see you for a minute?"

But Eugene didn't open the door. The yard and house were completely still, except for the twinkling lights flapping in the wind. Branches of the oak tree whipped around overhead. A small branch tore loose from the tree and flew into Eugene's yard.

"Come out!" Liza hollered. "We know who you are."

"You've ruined everything," Eddie bellowed.

"Shhh," Melody warned, "you'll make him mad."

"Maybe we should thank him for the wishes," Liza said. "After all, some of them did turn out good."

Howie shook his head. "Not one of them did. We've caused a terrible flood, half the school's sick from eating junk, and Mrs. Jeepers will probably lose her job for being too nice."

"And worst of all, Carey thinks I like her!" Eddie sputtered.

"Everything's a mess," Melody agreed. "And this storm will make it worse."

"Where is that bike-riding wish-giver?" Eddie asked. "He's always here after school."

"I don't think he can hear us over the wind," Liza said.

"Let's scream together," Howie told them.

"Eugene!" the four kids screamed. But the only answer was the whistling of the wind as it grew stronger and stronger.

Liza grabbed the fence when a huge gust of wind sent her scarf sailing into the branches of the oak tree, and paper from Melody's notebook flew in every direction. Howie looked up just in time to see a carpet flying past him. But he blinked, and then it was gone.

"This is crazy," Melody screamed as she crawled after her papers.

"We're going to be blown clear to Ruby Mountain," Liza wailed and squeezed the fence tighter. "This is all Eugene's fault."

Melody grabbed a piece of paper that was flying by and screamed, "I wish everything was back to normal!"

12

Four Genies

It was the next morning and the four kids could see the food delivery men unloading boxes of broccoli and corn dogs from their big white truck. The air was crisp and cool, and a thin layer of frost covered the ground. Under the frost, the kids could see litter scattered across the yard behind the school. The twinkling lights were gone, and so was Eugene.

"I guess things really are back to normal," Melody said.

Eddie nodded. "That windstorm really trashed the place up again."

"I thought we were going to be blown over the rainbow by that wind yesterday," Liza said.

"But we did it," Melody told them. "We saved Bailey City."

Howie nodded. "The cool weather has stopped the flood. The snow on Ruby Mountain is frozen again."

Eddie pulled his jacket tighter. "I'm glad my dad's company canceled his trip, even if they did take the sports car back."

Melody looked at the empty house. "I think I'm going to miss Eugene."

Howie agreed. "It's not every day you get to meet a real live genie."

"Even if he wasn't a genie, he sure made this old junky yard sparkle," Liza said.

"Hey, what's this?" Eddie yelled as he reached into the branches for a small brown bottle.

"Don't open it!" his friends screamed.

Eddie shook his head. "It's already open, and there's a note inside." The kids huddled around and read the strange handwriting.

It is within you
To make wishes come true

"It's from Eugene," Melody told them. "He's telling us we can make our wishes come true."

"Don't tell me you're turning into a genie!" Eddie slapped his forehead.

"Maybe just a little." Melody smiled. "After school I'm going to get some trash bags and clean up that yard myself."

"Are you crazy?" Eddie asked. "That's too much work."

"I'll help you." Liza smiled. "Maybe I have a little genie in me, too."

"Count me in," Howie told them. "Just don't open any strange-looking bottles."

The girls giggled and said together, "*No way!*" Then Melody, Liza, and Howie looked at Eddie.

"What about you?" Melody asked. "Will you help?"

Eddie bowed low. "Your wish is my command."

Debbie Dadey and Marcia Thornton Jones have fun writing stories together. When they both worked at an elementary school in Lexington, Kentucky, Debbie was the school librarian and Marcia was a teacher. During their lunch break in the school cafeteria, they came up with the idea of the Bailey School kids.

Recently Debbie and her family moved to Plano, Texas. Marcia and her husband still live in Kentucky where she continues to teach. How do these authors still write together? They talk on the phone and use computers and fax machines!